NANCY POCKET
AND THE
KIDNAPPERS

Julia Jarman

Illustrated by
JEAN BAYLIS

HEINEMANN · LONDON

Lauren

William Heinemann Ltd
Michelin House
81 Fulham Road
London SW3 6RB

LONDON   MELBOURNE   AUCKLAND

First published in 1991
Text © Julia Jarman 1991
Illustrations © Jean Baylis 1991
ISBN 0 434 97678 4

Printed in Italy
by Olivotto

A school pack of BANANA BOOKS 43-48 is
available from Heinemann Educational Books
ISBN 0 435 00107 8

Chapter One

NANCY POCKET LIVED with just her mum and dad at 5 Magnolia Avenue, and she liked it that way. It was a large house with a large garden. Nancy Pocket had a room of her own. In fact she had two. She had lots of books. She had lots of toys. She had a computer and an amiable cat called Cornflake – he was white with ginger

splodges – and she had a best friend called Tom. He collected skeletons.

Nancy Pocket lacked for nothing. Nor, she thought, did her mum and dad. So it was a bit of a shock, one Sunday morning, when Mrs Pocket said, 'I'm going to have a baby, Nancy Pocket. You're going to be a big sister. You'll like that.'

Nancy said nothing.

Quite soon her mum's lap grew so big and bumpy that Nancy couldn't sit on it any more. Then Mrs Pocket went into hospital. But when she came out again she didn't have one baby, she had three. THREE!

It's not fair, thought Nancy, I wasn't warned about this.

Nor it seemed were Mr and Mrs Pocket.

'Meet the Triplets,' said Nancy's dad. He looked dazed.

'We're going to need a lot of help,' said mum.

Nancy still said nothing.

Chapter Two

THE TRIPLETS LOOKED like squashed tomatoes. Nevertheless hundreds of people came to see them, including a reporter from the Camberly Post and a film crew from T.V. East. They appeared on the news, and in an advert for Nifty Nappies.

'Niffy more like,' said Nancy. 'Poo.'

'Nancy!' said Gran Pocket who had come to help.

'Gran!' said Nancy. 'They are disgusting and you know it.'

Mr and Mrs Pocket called them Simon, Susan and Peter. Nancy called them Soggy, Sicky and Pong. Gran Pocket said they would improve.

Soggy Simon was very squirty and left damp patches all over the house. Sicky Sue smelled of sour milk and made Mrs Pocket smell of sour milk too. Peter the Pong was, well, even pongier than the others. He got you-know-what EVERYWHERE, but he did have nice ears. Nancy had to admit, she liked his ears, especially when he was asleep. They were a bit velvety and a bit sticky-out, like Ted's.

But Ted didn't yell, and Peter the Pong

did. So did all the triplets, especially at
night. During the day, the washing
machine never stopped sloshing, the
tumble drier never stopped trundling –
and Mr and Mrs Pocket just never
stopped. It was 'Now now, Nancy,' all day
long. And there were buckets
everywhere, full of the most yukky
things.

Chapter Three

'IT'S TERRIBLE,' SHE said to Tom, when he called for a dead mouse for his collection. Cornflake had caught it.

'Try a clothes peg,' said Tom, who didn't mind smells or blood or bones.

'You don't understand,' said Nancy. Nobody did.

Things got worse as the triplets grew. They got louder for a start, though they still couldn't say anything sensible. And they started to move around. Like an invading army they advanced through the house. Nothing was safe.

First they crawled. Then they climbed. Then they threw things.

Cornflake went to live in the garage.

Nancy made a big notice for her bedroom door.

PRIVATE KEEP OUT.

But of course the triplets couldn't read.

One Thursday Nancy came home from school, and there was The Pong, in her room, and he'd broken her computer.

'You're a demon!' she shouted. 'A
devil. A monster! GET OUT!'

She dumped him on the landing. Then
she barricaded the door – with a chair and
some pillows and her dressing up box.

'Stay out of my room!'

'Waaaa . . . gh! Waaaa . . . gh!
Waaaa . . . gh!' He sounded like
Cornflake with his tail in the door.

*hollow tree by the pond in Abington Park
at midnight tonight. Do not tell the police.*

It was too late. The police were on their
way.

'We haven't got a million pounds,'
sobbed Mrs Pocket. 'I'll never see my
babies again.'

'Great,' thought Nancy, 'Fantastic. It
will be just like it used to be.'

But it wasn't. For a start the house was full of policemen. They told Mr and Mrs

Pocket to follow the kidnapper's instructions. So late that night her dad left the house. Nancy heard him. He was taking a million pounds – in fake notes – to the hollow tree in Abington Park. But later she heard him return – and he hadn't got the triplets. The kidnappers hadn't shown up. Mr Pocket thought they must have seen the policemen coming to the house.

Chapter Five

WHEN NANCY GOT up in the morning
her mum and dad weren't there, though
Gran was. Instead they were on Breakfast
T.V. begging the kidnappers to bring back
their babies. But they didn't.

Nancy had never seen her mum look so
sad. She hoped she would soon cheer up.

The police said it was a pity they hadn't
more clues. Mrs Pocket couldn't
remember much. It had all happened so
quickly, she said. She had just come in

from the shops. The triplets were still in their baby-buggy, when two men burst in. One of them grabbed the buggy and took it outside. The other had grabbed her and covered her eyes. Then he'd tied her up. She had fought hard she said. She knew she'd bitten her captor's finger. And when he'd gone she'd heard a vehicle driving away.

A vehicle? Two men. That jogged Nancy's memory. She remembered the

removal van and the men inside. But she didn't say anything. Why should she? The house was quiet again. She had her two rooms again. The house smelled nice again. Cornflake moved back indoors.

Best of all Mr and Mrs Pocket now had plenty of time for Nancy – almost too much. In fact they hardly let her out of their sight. They took her to school and they met her from school. And they didn't let her play with Tom so much.

'What if they come and kidnap you, Nancy Pocket? What would we do without you?'

They were utterly miserable without the triplets. And Nancy wasn't as happy as she thought she'd be.

She couldn't help thinking about the removal van – and the very loud music coming from it – to drown the cries of the triplets she supposed. How frightened they must have been.

Then, to make her feel worse, another ransom note arrived.

Pay up quickly or else. And no tricks this time. Leave the money in the litter bin in Pigeon Square at 12pm.
P.S. Half a million will do.

Attached to the note was a piece of each of the Triplet's hair. Nancy thought about the kidnapper's message. What did it mean? What terrible thing would they do next?

Tom came round to show Nancy his latest find – a crow's skull. But Nancy wasn't in the mood. She took one look and burst into tears.

'Cheer up, Nancy,' said Tom. 'The police will catch those men any day now.'

'But I want the triplets back,' cried Nancy. 'I want them NOW!'

Chapter Six

NANCY TOLD HER mum and dad about the removal van, that it had GREENS written on the side. Straightaway, her mum and dad told the police and a nationwide search began. Everyone praised Nancy for remembering, but that made her feel worse.

Mr and Mrs Pocket tried to comfort her. 'The police are doing their best,' they said.

'They're not fast enough,' said Nancy.

'They need help,' said Tom. 'Why don't we keep a look-out?'

'Be detectives, you mean? That's only in books,' said Nancy.

But Tom tried, he really did. The very next day he thought he'd found them, but it was just a day nursery he'd never noticed before. There were hundreds of nappies in the garden. And the day after that he followed a red and white baby buggy all the way home from school, only to find there were twins in it, not triplets.

Nancy felt worse and worse. She had tummy ache all the time, didn't feel like eating. How bad she was. But then something happened which turned her into a real detective! Brought her face to face with the criminals themselves!

She had gone to stay with Gran Pocket, because her mum and dad thought she needed a holiday. And it was there in Bexley Heath that she saw the kidnappers!

She was in a supermarket at the time – on her own because Gran had sprained her ankle.

'Buy some things that you like,' Gran had said. And Nancy was putting frankfurters and alphabet spaghetti into the trolley when she saw them.

Two men in the next alley. Immediately her suspicions were aroused. They didn't look a bit like fathers, and they were piling baby food into their trolley, which was already half full of nappies. One of the men was fat with hairy nostrils, the other looked a bit like a thistle. He had a bristly chin and stand-up hair. And Hairy Nostrils had a bandaged finger! Where mum bit him, thought Nancy. That proves it.

Her heart was thumping. She knew she must follow them, get their car number at least, their address if possible. But what if they recognised her? She needed a disguise. She dodged behind a pile of baked beans, delved into her bag and brought out Gran's raincoat and hat. Keeping watch, she put them both on, pulling the hat over her eyes. Did she look like a little old woman? She hoped so.

Somebody gave her a funny look. But the men were at the checkout now. She had to follow them. She went to the checkout next to theirs. Unloaded. Paid. Loaded into her bag.

The men were just ahead of her. She followed them to the car park – this was dodgy – and they stopped by a rusty blue Cortina.

She stopped – behind a red Mini and watched Hairy Nostrils open the car door, driver's side. She saw him go to the boot and try to open it. It stuck. He swore.

Thistle-Head said, 'Let me have a go, you cack-handed gump.'

And while their eyes were on the boot, Nancy took her chance – for Hairy Nostrils had left the side door open! She dashed forward, pushed up the driver's seat, dived into the back of the car and pulled the seat back again. Immediately she regretted what she'd done. Why hadn't she simply gone to the police? But it was too late now. If she tried to get out they would be sure to see her. So she crouched on the floor, her heart thumping so loudly that she couldn't hear what was happening.

Would they manage to open the boot?
Could they see her through the back
window? If they decided to put the things
on the back seat she was done for.

The boot slammed shut. They were
coming. They got in the front and
slammed the doors.

The engine whirred, chugged, juddered.
More swearing, more whirring, then the

car jerked forward with a roar. But where to? Where were they going? And what would she do when she got there?

'Step on it,' Hairy-Nostrils was worried too. 'If the brats wake up and start screaming we're in trouble.'

Brats? How dare they? And surely they hadn't left the triplets on their own?

Outside it was getting dark and the traffic was building up. That was all she could tell. The car stopped and started – for traffic lights she supposed, and sometimes it didn't start. The men got angrier. Thistle-Head said they needed a new car. Nostrils said they'd get one – when the Pockets paid up.

Thistle-Head said, 'What if they don't then? Tell me that. What if they don't want 'em back? I wouldn't.'

Nostrils said, 'Shut your mouth.'

Chapter Seven

SOON AFTER THAT the car stopped and the men got out. Nancy heard them opening the boot. Closing it. Walking away. Now what? She risked a peep and saw the men disappearing into a block of flats. She opened the car door and raced across the pavement to the entrance. They'd gone – but a lift was going up. She watched the numbers . . . 3 . . 4 . . 5 .. . . 8. Stop.

She pressed the button marked LIFT and waited for it to come down.

She waited and waited. Pressed again. Then started to climb the stairs.

At least she had time to think. Eighth floor she knew that, but what door number? And how would she get the triplets out of the flat? How would she get inside? The higher she climbed, the harder her task seemed – and she was just about to go down again and phone the police after all, when she heard a baby crying. It was a miserable, frightened cry – and it spurred her on to the next landing. Clearly it was coming from Number 97.

'Shurrup!'

'Stick summat in his gob. D'ye want the neighbours to hear?'

Smash! Nancy pressed the fire alarm.

Bells rang and doors opened, including Number 97's.

'Spect it's some kid.'

It wasn't. It was a little old lady in a rain hat.

'The boiler room,' said the little old lady. 'It's on fire.'

'Don't use the lift,' said someone, 'it's dangerous in a fire.'

'Let's get out of here,' said someone else.

There was a stampede for the stairs. Down they all went – all except the kidnappers.

'Shall I give you a hand with the babies?' said the little old lady. She could see them through the open door –

strapped in their buggy. They smelled awful and Peter was crying.

But the kidnappers scarpered. So Nancy walked right in.

'Sh. It's me, Nancy,' she said.

Peter stopped crying, but Simon and Susan started. Quickly she pushed them out of the door. She could hear the kidnappers clattering down the stairs. Good riddance.

She pressed the LIFT button – and up it came. She got in – with the triplets of course. DOWN . . 7 . . 6 . . 5 . . .

Her heart was still thudding but it was beginning to look as if she would make it, though the triplets were still screaming . . 4 . . 3 . . 2.

She took off her hat.

'Look, it's me Nancy.'

Simon and Susan screamed louder.

'Ancy,' said Peter. He smiled.

'You'll soon be home now.'

As soon as she saw a telephone box she would ring the police. They arrived at the ground floor. She pressed OPEN. The doors opened . . . and there were the kidnappers, blocking her exit.

'I told you it were 'er,' said Thistle-Head.

'And there ain't no fire,' said Hairy Nostrils. 'So back you go before anyone sees you.'

He pushed her – and Nancy rammed the buggy against his shins. He pushed

her again but Nancy pressed the CLOSE
button. And there was Hairy Nostrils
with his head trapped between the lift
doors.

Nancy kept her finger on the button
until she heard a voice say, 'Let go now,
love. This is the fire brigade.'

'Don't let this man go,' said Nancy.
'He's a kidnapper.'

Then the doors opened and there were
three firemen and one firewoman holding
Hairy Nostrils in a half-nelson.

Thistle-Head ran for the main door.
'Get him too!' yelled Nancy, just as a
police dog jumped out and caught him by
the trouser-leg.

The police took the kidnappers away in
handcuffs. Then Nancy and the triplets
went home in the fire engine, and
everybody cheered as they arrived.

Later, Tom said the best bit must have been appearing on television. Nancy had to tell all the viewers how she'd rescued the triplets. But *she* said the best bit was having them home again.

Tom said, 'You're kidding? Even the pong and the mess and not having your two rooms?'

And Nancy said, 'Yup.'

It was amazing, but she meant it. She really did.